Books should be returned or renewed by the last date above. Renew by phone **08458 247 200** or online *www.kent.gov.uk/libs*

Libraries & Archives

CUSTOMER SERVICE EXCELLENCE

The Government Standard

Kent County Council

01128\DTP\RN\11.10   LIB 7

For Tom ~ H.W.
For Jennie and Sam ~ K.P.

WOOF

magazine

STRIPES PUBLISHING
An imprint of Magi Publications
1 The Coda Centre,
189 Munster Road,
London SW6 6AW

A paperback original
First published in Great Britain
in 2011

Text copyright © Holly Webb, 2011
Illustrations copyright
© Kate Pankhurst, 2011
Cover photographs copyright
© Lifeonwhite.com, 2011

ISBN: 978-1-84715-165-0

The right of Holly Webb and Kate Pankhurst to be identified as the author and illustrator of this work respectively has been asserted by them in accordance with the Copyright, Designs and Patents Act, 1988.

A CIP catalogue record for this book is available from the British Library.

Printed and bound in the UK.

10 9 8 7 6 5 4 3 2 1

My Naughty Little Puppy

Holly Webb

Illustrated by
Kate Pankhurst

Stripes

Chapter One

Exciting News

"Off the lead training..." Ellie murmured, looking down at Rascal and chewing her bottom lip. He was in a very bouncy mood this evening, and so far he'd tripped her up in walking to heel, and managed to snatch the whole bag of dog treats she'd brought to give him if he was good. She'd had to borrow some spare ones from her friend Jack. Jack's enormous Great Dane puppy, Hugo, was looking quite annoyed.

My Naughty Little Puppy

Reluctantly, Ellie undid Rascal's lead. They hadn't been doing off the lead work for very long, but Rascal had been starting to get the hang of it. He just didn't seem to be in the mood to behave today... She glanced anxiously over at Dad. Dad gave her a thumbs up, and Ellie tried to look confident. Their instructor, Jo, was always saying that if they were nervous, their puppies would pick up on it and be naughty.

Rascal wagged his tail happily as Ellie unclipped his lead. They were supposed to be practising recalling the puppies, so Ellie let him wander off to weave in and out of his big friend Hugo's legs, and then called, "Rascal!"

My Naughty Little Puppy

She smiled with relief as Rascal turned immediately, and pattered back to her, looking hopeful. "Good boy!" she told him happily, giving him one of Hugo's treats. "Well done!" Just then, Ellie noticed out of the corner of her eye that Amelia, who was in Year Six at her school and was always rude about Rascal, wasn't doing so well. Her pretty little spaniel, Goldie, had got into a scrap with one of the other dogs, and was completely ignoring Amelia. Ellie tried not to look smug as she sent Rascal off again.

Then she put her hand to her mouth in horror. They'd taken Rascal for a run round the park before dog training – Jo had suggested they always did that, so the puppies could do a wee before they came into the class. But obviously Rascal had had a lot to drink today. He was looking around thoughtfully in a way that Ellie recognized...

"Rascal! No, wait!"

Ellie blushed scarlet and rushed over, but she was too late to stop Rascal lifting his leg against one of the big old radiators that kept the village hall warm in the winter. He left rather a large puddle, and Ellie could hear Amelia sniggering behind her.

"Oh, dear!" Jo came over. "I'll nip and get you some kitchen roll, Ellie!"

Ellie nodded, crouching down next to Rascal so as not to see everyone else giggling. "Oh, Rascal," she muttered. "And we were doing so well!"

"Don't worry, Ellie. No one minded," Dad said soothingly, as they walked home, but Ellie still felt embarrassed. When was Rascal going to become one of those perfectly trained dogs, like Jo's golden Labrador, Emma?

They let themselves into the house, and Rascal raced into the kitchen to see if anything had magically appeared in his food bowl since he last looked.

Mum, Lila and Max were sitting at the kitchen table, and Mum had paper and a pen in front of her. She was clearly making one of her "lists", and Ellie sighed. Mum liked lists, but they always meant lots of work for everyone else.

"So you need to make sure that any clothes you want to take are in the basket, so I can get them washed before it's time to pack. Oh, you too, Ellie."

"Pack for what?" Ellie asked.

"We're going to Gran and Grandpa's! Gran just rang up and said it was definitely OK!" Max told her excitedly.

"Really? Brilliant!" Ellie beamed. Their grandparents lived by the sea, in a little

town called Green Bay. It was a proper
old-fashioned seaside place, with gorgeous
sandy beaches, a pier and the best fish
and chip shop ever. "Hey! It'll be the first
time Rascal's been to the seaside! I bet he'll
love it. When are we going, Mum?"

My Naughty Little Puppy

"The first week of the summer holiday –
so straight after you break up from school
at the end of the week," Mum said, but
she was looking worried. "Ellie, I'm not
absolutely sure we're going to take Rascal..."

Ellie stared at her. "But we have to! We
can't just leave him behind."

"No, of course not, but he might have
to go to kennels. You know how fussy
Gran can be – she worries about the mess
you and Lila and Max make, let alone a
puppy."

Ellie felt like crying. She had been
imagining showing Rascal all her favourite
places in Green Bay. Maybe he'd even
want to go in the sea with her! "I don't
want to go without him..." she said, her

voice all sniffly. "Please, Mum! He'd hate being in kennels, away from all of us."

"It's true, Mum," Lila put in. "He'd be really miserable." Max nodded too.

"I know." Mum got up and gave Ellie a hug. "I'll talk to Gran about it. After all, Rascal's so much better behaved now, isn't he? Was he good at training tonight?"

Ellie swallowed, and glanced over at Dad. "Well, most of the time..."

Chapter Two

Last Day

Mum was still really unsure about taking Rascal on holiday, especially after Ellie had told her about him weeing during dog training. She'd phoned Gran, and they'd talked about it for ages, while Ellie had sat on the stairs listening, and watching Rascal rolling over and over down the hallway with his squeaky bone. He was so cute - how could Gran not love him?

Ellie told her best friend Christy all about

My Naughty Little Puppy

it as they waited in the playground for the morning bell on Friday - the last day before the holidays.

"Mum said that Gran's agreed, but she's still really not keen on having a puppy to stay, so we'll all have to make sure he behaves," she explained.

My Naughty Little Puppy

Everyone was tearing round excitedly, making sure they all had phone numbers for meeting up during the summer. Ellie, Christy and their friend Lucy had clubbed together and bought a lovely mug with dogs on for their teacher, Mrs Harley, who liked dogs too. They were going to give it to her at the end of school.

"I bet your gran will like him when she gets to know him," said Christy.

Ellie sighed. She hoped so, but she just wasn't sure. Gran was one of those people who always looked perfect – her hair was styled like she'd just come out of the hairdresser, and she never, ever spilt anything on her clothes. Her house was the same – always tidy, with a lot of small and very breakable china ornaments dotted around. It really wasn't the best sort of place to take Rascal. "She's just not a dog person..." Ellie said. "But at least we'll be out on the beach most of the time, so he won't be getting under her feet."

"Actually, that's a good idea," Christy agreed. "Why don't you take him for loads of long walks along the beach? That way, he'll be too tired to be naughty."

Ellie smiled. "Good plan, and I'm going to try and get him to come swimming with me. That'll definitely wear him out. Jo said that Jack Russells usually love swimming. I'm just so glad Gran said yes in the end. He would have hated going to kennels, and I'd really miss him!"

Christy nodded. "Bouncer's going to stay with my uncle when we go away to France. We did send him to kennels once, but he was really grumpy when we picked him up. He went down to the end of the garden and sulked for a whole day."

Ellie giggled. Bouncer was Christy's gorgeous golden Labrador, and he was so happy and friendly that she couldn't imagine him having a strop.

"You're really lucky getting to take Rascal with you," Christy said enviously. "You'll have such a good time."

"I should think Rascal would probably tear a boarding kennel apart," Ellie said, shuddering. "He'd be banned from kennels for life!"

My Naughty Little Puppy

There were already bags and bags piled up in the hallway when Ellie and Max got home from school, and Mum was looking a bit harassed. "Hello, you two! Ellie, I've just looked in your room, and you haven't even started packing! You do know we're going early tomorrow morning, don't you?"

Ellie nodded. "It's OK, Mum, I'll go and do it now." She stuck her school bag in the cupboard under the stairs – she didn't even have to think about school for six whole weeks! Then she raced upstairs to pull out her suitcase from under the bed and decide what she was taking.

Rascal dashed up the stairs after her,

although it took him a bit longer – his legs
were a lot shorter than Ellie's, and he had
to scrabble for every step.

"Oh! Sorry, Rascal!" Ellie came halfway
down again to pick him up. "I'm just really
excited about going on holiday! I mustn't
forget to pack for you, too. Your dog-bed,
and your bowls – we'll take the nice ones
I painted for you; I want to show them to
Gran. And lots of food and dog treats and
your toys." She frowned. "I hope Dad's
remembered he'll need space in the car for
all your stuff, and you in your pet carrier."

Ellie's suitcase was full long before she
had fitted in all the stuff she thought she'd
need, and then Mum pointed out that she
hadn't packed any pyjamas, and she had

to take everything out and start again.
It took ages, and Rascal got bored halfway
through and went back downstairs. At last,
Ellie sat down on her suitcase, and just
about managed to zip it up.

She sighed happily and eyed the pile of stuff that was still on her bed. Mum might not agree that it was better to take just one cardigan and fit in six books and her favourite pencils, but it would be OK if Ellie didn't tell her.

She raced down the stairs, making for the kitchen. She was sure she could smell tomato pasta sauce, and she was starving. But she stopped dead in the hallway, staring at the pile of stuff that was waiting to go in the car.

Rascal was curled up fast asleep inside Max's yellow fishing net. It probably still smelled of the crabs Max had used it to catch the last time they'd been to the seaside, Ellie realized as she went closer.

She didn't think Rascal had ever had crab – it wasn't a popular flavour for dog food. But he seemed to like it – or maybe it was just that the net was nice and chewy. At any rate, it now had several extra holes.

"Rascal!" Ellie cried. She had a feeling that her holiday money wouldn't last very long. There was no way she was going to convince Max that nets were meant to have holes that big in them!

Chapter Three

A Nightmare Journey

"Right! It's all in, just about. Come on, let's get going." Dad was looking pleased with himself, and Ellie thought he deserved to be, after managing to squash that huge pile of stuff into the car.

"I hope Rascal's going to be OK," she said to Mum, as she picked him up and went over to his pet carrier. "He's never been on a long car journey before."

Mum tickled Rascal behind the ears.

My Naughty Little Puppy

"I'm sure he'll be fine. It's only an hour and
a half, and he doesn't mind the car, now,
does he? He's been fine when we've driven
to the woods. He'll probably just go to
sleep after a while."

Ellie slipped Rascal into his pet carrier,
which was surrounded by bags and boxes.
He stood there looking rather confused.
He didn't go in the car very often, and
he'd certainly never seen it this full. Dad
had made sure he could see out, but it had
been tricky.

My Naughty Little Puppy

"It's OK," Ellie told him. "It won't take that long to get there, and we're going to have the best time."

But an hour later, Ellie felt like the journey was never going to end. It was all Max's fault for bringing an enormous bag of fizzy chews. Ellie was sure that they were all fizzing away in her stomach, and she felt awful. Wriggling herself round to keep checking on Rascal hadn't helped either.

"Are we nearly there?" she asked Dad, in a wobbly voice.

"About another half-hour." Mum looked round at her. "Oh, Ellie, you're very pale. Are you all right?"

"I feel sick..." Ellie moaned.

"Don't be sick anywhere near me!"

My Naughty Little Puppy

Lila squeaked. "These are my new jeans!"

There was a funny little moaning noise from the boot behind them, and Max turned round to peer at Rascal. "Oh, dear. I don't think Rascal's feeling so good either," he reported. "He's just lying there, and he looks miserable."

My Naughty Little Puppy

Dad sighed. "Well, I would stop to let you all get some fresh air, but I think if we allowed Rascal out of his pet carrier, we might never get him back in again. We really won't be long. Can you hold on, Ellie?"

Ellie groaned, and Dad sped up a bit.

Twenty minutes later, Max yelled, "Look, I can see the sea! And there's a sign for Green Bay."

"Hurry up, Dad!" Ellie wailed. "I really think I'm going to be sick!"

Rascal joined in with more sad moaning noises from the boot.

"We're just coming to Gran and Grandpa's road now," Dad promised.

He pulled up in front of a pretty cottage. "OK! Everybody out!"

Ellie stumbled out of the car and leaned against the front fence, trying very hard not to throw up. "Never, ever give me those things again," she told Max, who looked unfairly bouncy and not carsick at all.

Max grinned at her, and waved the bag under her nose.

"Ugh!" Ellie wailed. "You're so mean! Mum, is Rascal OK?"

Dad had just opened the boot to start unloading the bags, and Mum was undoing Rascal's pet carrier. "He doesn't look very happy..."

Ellie went over to help her. She was

starting to feel a tiny bit better now she
wasn't in the car any more.

"Hey, Rascal..." Rascal lifted his head off
his paws and gazed glumly up at Ellie. "Oh,
you really do look sick. Come on, let's get
you out. Look, there's Gran and Grandpa
coming to see us!"

She lifted Rascal out of the car, clipped
on his lead, and led him over to the front
gate, where her grandparents were just
heading down the path. She smiled happily
at Gran and Grandpa – their house was
so like them, old-fashioned and perfectly
tidy. All the flowers in the front garden were
in beautiful neat rows, and Grandpa had
the shortest, most velvety lawn Ellie had
ever seen.

My Naughty Little Puppy

"Hello, sweetheart!" Gran was just coming forward to give Ellie a hug, when Rascal stopped dead in the gateway, and was sick all over Gran's path.

"Oh!" Gran stared down at Rascal like he was some horrible sort of beetle, and Grandpa laughed. "Poor little chap. Did he not like the car, Ellie?"

Ellie shook her head, wishing she and Rascal could go and hide. "I'm really sorry!" she wailed. "He never usually does that!"

Gran smiled, but Ellie could tell she was making a real effort not to be grumpy. "Never mind. We'll put some sand over it and clean it up later. Come and have some tea, all of you!" She paused for a moment. "Bring the puppy too, Ellie..."

My Naughty Little Puppy

After the sick incident, Mum decided it would be best if Ellie got Rascal out of the way for a bit, so she sent her and Max down to the beach with Dad, while she and Lila stayed to unpack and help Gran clean the path.

The gorgeous, tangy sea air soon blew away Ellie's carsickness, and it seemed to have cheered up Rascal, too. Gran's house was just at the end of the road from the beach, and he stood at the top of the cliff path staring down at the sea, his tail a waggy blur of excitement. They rushed down the steep steps, and suddenly Ellie almost didn't care that Rascal had thrown

up right in front of Gran, it was just so
exciting to see the sea!

The summer holidays had only just
begun so there weren't very many people
on the beach. It was a long stretch of
biscuity-looking golden-brown sand, with
sweeps of pebbles here and there. Ellie
looked around thoughtfully, and unclipped
Rascal's lead.

"Do you want to explore? Off you go!"
she suggested, and
Rascal dashed
off at once, his
nose to the
sand, sniffing
eagerly at all the
interesting smells.

Ellie followed him, laughing to herself at how excited he was. He tracked across the sand towards the sea, and then pulled up short, staring at the strange greenish-grey water ... that was coming towards him!

"It's OK." Ellie crouched down next to him. "It's just the sea. It does that." She slipped off her flip-flops, and paddled in the seawater, wincing a little at the cold.

Rascal watched her curiously, and poked one paw towards the sea. It looked like water... It smelled a little strange, but he was very, very thirsty. As the tide crept in towards his paws, he leaned down and lapped at it, and then spat it out disgustedly.

He backed away, looking horrified. What was that stuff? It didn't taste like

My Naughty Little Puppy

water. He barked sharply to tell Ellie not to drink any. He wasn't sure about this at all.

"Come on. It's fun, look," said Ellie, splashing about in the waves. But Rascal stayed safely on the sand where he was.

Chapter Four

Cat-astrophe!

"I think it's lunchtime," Dad said, looking at his watch. "Shall we go back home?"

Ellie looked anxious. She hoped Gran wasn't still cross with Rascal. And she'd been planning to impress her with how beautifully trained he was, too!

But Gran seemed to have recovered - she even patted Rascal and said how sweet he was, and Grandpa thought he was great. Ellie demonstrated how well Rascal

would stay, sometimes even with a biscuit between his paws, and Grandpa was very impressed. Ellie was pretty sure she saw him feeding Rascal a sandwich crust under the table when Gran wasn't looking, too.

After lunch, Grandpa took them outside to show off his garden. Ellie loved it. It wasn't very big, but it was full of secret corners and surprises. Ellie always liked the family of stone frogs – Grandpa moved them around the garden, and when she was little, she was sure they'd moved by themselves when she wasn't looking.

Rascal loved it too, and he pottered around investigating the earthy garden smells. Then all at once he noticed a new smell – a cat smell! His tail started to wag excitedly. He hadn't met that many cats, but there was something about them that simply made him want to give chase. There it was! A huge ginger tom cat was sitting on the stone bench on the other side of the little lawn, washing its paws.

Rascal sprang across the grass, barking so loudly that Ellie put her hands over her ears. Then she spotted the cat too. "Oh, Rascal, no!" she gasped.

My Naughty Little Puppy

"It's that dratted cat from two doors down," Grandpa said. "Nasty fat thing, it's always pouncing on the birds on our feeders."

But Ellie wasn't listening. She was chasing Rascal, who was chasing the cat – down off the bench, round behind the rose bushes, across the patio, and up on to the little wall that ran along the edge of the paving.

My Naughty Little Puppy

At least, the cat went up on to the
wall... Rascal scrabbled desperately with
his front paws, and barked and barked,
but it was no good, he couldn't follow it
up there. The cat gave him an insolent
stare and jumped from the wall to the
fence, and down into next-door's garden.

"Whatever is going on?" Gran came
out of the kitchen door. "I could hear the
barking all the way upstairs!"

Just then, there was a big crash. Rascal
had knocked over a pretty pot of flowers!

Gran gasped, and Ellie
put her hands over her
mouth in horror. Grandpa's
beautiful flowers! Now he
would be furious with Rascal too!

My Naughty Little Puppy

"Oh, you bad dog!" Gran scolded.

"No, no, it wasn't the little pup's fault,"
Grandpa said, patting Rascal, who was
standing with his tail between his legs.
"It was that dratted ginger cat. Rascal was
just doing what dogs do..."

"Hmph," Gran muttered. And Ellie was
almost sure that as she turned away to go
back into the house, she added, "I just wish
he wasn't doing it here!"

"Never mind, Ellie." Grandpa gave her
a hug. "I was getting bored with those
petunias anyway. I'll nip down to the garden
centre later and buy some new flowers."

Ellie managed a small smile, but inside
she felt miserable. Gran was never going
to like Rascal now!

Chapter Five

One Wet Dog

Ellie and Lila were sharing the little bedroom in the attic of Gran and Grandpa's house, and the next morning Ellie was woken early by the bright sun shining in through the tiny window above her head.

"Lila!" she whispered. Ellie was always careful with Lila in the mornings. If she growled, it would be best to leave her alone. But Lila just made a sleepy sort of sighing noise.

"Lila, wake up, it's really sunny. Do you want to take Rascal down to the beach?"

"What time is it?" Lila groaned.

"Um, seven."

"Elli-eeee! It's the holidays!"

"But it's so sunny and lovely out! Look!" Ellie pulled open the curtains and peered out of the little window. "Oh, Lila, the sea's all sparkly!" She went over and perched on the end of Lila's bed. "Please, Lila! I want to take Rascal to the beach and make him run around for ages to wear him out. I've got to get him to behave better. What if Gran says she just can't have him in the house for a whole week? We might have to go home!"

Lila sat up. "She wouldn't!"

Ellie shook her head. "You didn't see

My Naughty Little Puppy

her after Rascal messed up the garden
yesterday. He's been nothing but trouble
since we got here."

"OK. Just give me a minute to work out
what I'm going to wear."

Ellie sighed. That meant at least twenty minutes. But Mum and Dad wouldn't be too happy about her and Rascal going to the beach on their own. She needed someone – and Max was even worse to get out of bed in the morning.

Lila was obviously worried about Gran and Rascal too, because she was ready fifteen minutes later, in her favourite pink denim shorts.

The girls crept downstairs, and Ellie fed Rascal while Lila wrote a note for Mum and Dad. Then they set off down the road to the sea.

A couple of old ladies stopped to admire Rascal, and he sat beautifully and let them stroke him. Ellie sighed as they walked

away, talking about how lovely he was.
If only he'd behave that nicely for Gran!

"There's people in the sea already!" Ellie
said, as they reached the top of the steps.

"It'll be cold this early in the morning."
Lila shivered. "I might go in later though."

There was a sign attached to the
railings. Ellie nudged Lila. "A sandcastle
competition! That's tomorrow, isn't it? We
should definitely do that. I'm sure Max will
want to join in too – he loves competitions."

Lila nodded. "It could be fun."

Rascal was pulling on his lead, wanting to get down on to the sand. "OK, OK!" Ellie laughed. "Come on then." As soon as they got to the beach she let him off his lead, and he raced up and down, sniffing at all the interesting bits and pieces that the sea had left behind, and every so often digging a hole to bury the best things.

Ellie looked at the water, trying to work out whether the tide was coming in or going out. "Be careful, Rascal," she told him. "It's coming in, I think."

Rascal wasn't listening. He trotted along the tide line, his nose rooting among the clumps of seaweed, old bits of rope, and empty crab shells. Ellie followed him,

looking for pretty shells – she was thinking
of sticking them on to a photo frame, to give
to Christy as part of her birthday present.
Lila was a little way off down the beach,
sitting on a big rock and enjoying the sun.

Suddenly, Rascal gave a surprised sort
of snuffle, and Ellie looked up. He was
staring down at a pile of seaweed, his ears
pricked up sharply, and his tail wagging.

"What is it?" Ellie asked. "Oh, a crab!
Is it still alive? You'd better leave it alone,
Rascal."

My Naughty Little Puppy

Rascal leaned forward, nose to nose
with the crab, his tail wagging faster and
faster. It wriggled! And scuttled! He followed
it along excitedly, and gave it a good sniff.
Then he leaped back with a yelp as the
crab nipped at his nose.

"Rascal, are you all right?"

Rascal was whimpering, and trying to
paw at his sore nose. He kept edging
backwards away from the crab, into the
wetter sand just at the edge of the water.

Ellie ran after him, but then she gasped
as Rascal backed straight into the path of a
wave. "Oh, watch out! Rascal, come here!"

It was only a little wave, but Rascal was
only a little dog, and it broke right over his
head. He ran out of the water, squeaking

with shock and shaking it out of his ears.

"Oh, Rascal!" Ellie swept him up and hugged him, and Rascal shook himself in her arms, getting her all wet too. "I did try to warn you. Poor boy."

From the safety of Ellie's arms, Rascal glared down at the water. He was now sure he didn't like that stuff at all.

Chapter Six

Sand Sand Sand!

Just as Ellie had thought, Max was keen to take part in the sandcastle competition, and they headed down to the beach the next morning armed with their buckets and spades.

"What shall we make?" Max asked. "I know – a pirate ship! That would be great, I bet we'll win if we do a pirate ship."

Lila shrugged. "Oh, fine then! I still think we ought to do a proper big castle. I'm off for a swim, anyway." She stalked away.

My Naughty Little Puppy

Ellie frowned. She had wondered about making a mermaid, but she knew what Max would have to say about that. She was pretty sure that the two red-haired boys with the little white Westie puppy that Rascal had barked at earlier were making a pirate ship. But Max was already drawing an outline in the sand with his spade, and it was too hot to argue. She started to dig, and Rascal scampered over to join in.

"Don't let Rascal do that, Ellie!" Max told her. "He'll ruin it!"

"He just likes digging," Ellie explained. "I'll try, though. Rascal! Come and dig here, look!" She started a hole for him with her spade, close to Mum and Dad's rug. That way Mum could keep half an eye on him

while she was reading her book. Rascal
dug eagerly, scraping away at the sand
with his paws, and Ellie went back to
helping Max.

My Naughty Little Puppy

Max had just sent Ellie off to look for sticks to be the masts, when Lila came dripping out of the sea, calling for her towel. "Ellie, can you pass it to me, I'm freezing!"

"But it isn't here..." Ellie looked around. "Did you take it down to the sea?"

"No, I left it here." Lila was standing by the rug now, dripping seawater on Mum. "Where's it gone?" She frowned, suddenly staring at Rascal, who was sitting on the sand by the rug and looking like an angel dog. It always meant he'd done something wrong, and Ellie eyed him anxiously.

"Oh no!" Lila wailed. "Look! He's buried my towel, I can see the end sticking out!"

Trying not to laugh, Ellie shooed Rascal out of the way and pulled up the sandy towel, trying to brush it off before she gave it to Lila.

"Uuurgh," Lila moaned, and Rascal yapped crossly. He'd just spent ages burying that! "Bad dog!" Lila snapped, leaning down and staring at him. "Naughty Rascal!"

"Come on, Rascal! Let's go and help Max," Ellie said hurriedly, as Lila stomped off to get dressed.

"What do you think, Ellie? It's nearly finished." Max looked down at their creation proudly. "I just want to add a few shells and things for the finishing touches. It isn't long till the judging."

"It looks great." Ellie crouched down to admire the piles of stones that Max had arranged to look like cannonballs next to his stick cannons.

Rascal sniffed thoughtfully at the strips of seaweed that Max had laid around the edges of the ship like waves.

Max looked up, and was just starting to say, "Don't..." when the little Westie

puppy wandered past, and sniffed the
seaweed too.

Rascal looked up, his ears bristling, and
barked sharply.

The Westie barked back, then decided
that Rascal was bigger than he was, and
ran back to his owners. But Rascal gave
chase, hurtling after the little white puppy –
straight through the middle of the almost-
finished pirate ship.

"I don't believe it..." Max growled.
"Just wait till I catch him!"

"We can fix it," Ellie said hopefully.

"No we can't, Ellie. Look at it! I'll go and tell the lady in charge we aren't entering any more."

"We could make something else quickly," Lila suggested, coming to look.

Max muttered something, and went to sulk on the rug.

"We should still enter," Lila said firmly. "Hey, what if we make a sand Rascal?"

Ellie and Lila started to pile up the sand so it looked like Rascal lying down. They added stones for eyes and a nose, a flat strip of seaweed for a collar and a pink shell for his tongue.

My Naughty Little Puppy

"That looks really good!" Dad said, coming over to see.

"It just needs another something," Lila said thoughtfully. "Where's Rascal? I need to see the real thing!"

Rascal scampered over to her and yapped happily, dropping one of Max's stick masts at her feet.

"That's it!" Ellie yelped. "Rascal, can we have it? Good boy! Look, Lila." She placed the stick carefully in front of the sand paws, as if Rascal was just lying down to chew at it.

"Perfect!" A lady with a clipboard was standing by them, laughing. "You finished just in time, didn't you? I like it, yes..." She made a scribble on her clipboard, and walked on to the sandy pyramid that some children had built nearby.

Max came over and stood next to Ellie and Lila, looking gloomy. "I suppose it's all right. It'll never win though."

"Shhh!" Lila hushed him. "Look, she's going to announce the winners."

"Third prize, the Larkin family."

"That's those boys with the other pirate ship," Max groaned. "I wonder what they won?"

The second prize went to the pyramid, and then the lady with the clipboard announced, "And the first prize goes to the Thomas family, for their lovely sand dog!"

"We won!" Ellie cried excitedly, and she and Lila went up to collect their prize.

"It's vouchers for the fish and chip shop," the lady explained, handing Ellie the prize. "Enjoy them!"

My Naughty Little Puppy

Lila and Ellie ran back to Mum and Dad. "Can we have fish and chips for lunch?" Ellie asked Mum. "It might cheer Max up," she added in a whisper.

"Fish and chips?" Max asked, breaking out of his sulk.

The fish and chip shop was further along the beach, just at the top of the cliff. It had picnic tables outside, and it was already getting full. Mum went to order, and soon came back with huge plates, piled with delicious-looking fish and chips. "Well done, Ellie and Lila," she said, smiling and lifting up a chip. "Mmmm!"

"And Rascal," Ellie pointed out. "We wouldn't have won without our model. Can he have a chip, Mum?" Rascal was sitting

up on his hind legs, waving his front paws
in the air. People at the other tables were
pointing him out and smiling. He did look
so cute when he begged like that.

"I suppose, just one..."

Rascal gobbled it down, and sat there in
the sun, while Ellie sneaked him a couple
more. Chips were definitely his new
favourite food...

Chapter Seven

A Picnic for Rascal

"Oh, look, it's that horrible cat again!" Gran waved the dishcloth crossly, as she looked through the kitchen window, and Ellie, who was helping her wash up after breakfast, stood on tiptoe to look out too.

"He's going to pounce on that blackbird," Ellie said, her voice squeaking with horror. She ran to the door. "Rascal, you stop him!"

Rascal didn't need asking twice. He shot out of the door as soon as Ellie opened it

for him, and raced down the garden, barking. The blackbird fluttered away in surprise, never knowing the danger it had been in, and the cat hissed at Rascal, its tail fluffing up to three times its size.

Ellie stared out of the door worriedly. The cat was bigger than Rascal and she hoped he wouldn't get hurt. She winced as the cat lashed out with one paw – she could see the claws from here!

But the scratch across his nose had Rascal jumping up and down and barking his head off, and the cat seemed to realize that now he meant business. It shot off up the fence, scrabbling and wobbling all the way to the top, then disappeared into next-door's garden with a last angry hiss.

Rascal barked at the fence for a little
while, in case the cat was thinking of
returning, and then trotted proudly back
to the kitchen.

Ellie watched him open-mouthed.
"Rascal, you were so brave! Oh, Gran,
look, that horrible cat scratched his nose."

"Nasty beast. Who's a good boy then?

Here, Rascal, you have this bit of leftover bacon." Gran gently wiped Rascal's scratch with a clean dishcloth, and Ellie beamed to herself.

"I was thinking we might take a picnic lunch down to the cove," Gran suggested. "I've got a special sponge cake tucked away in the cupboard and I'll make up some sandwiches. It's lovely for swimming there, and we've never taken you children. Just you and me and Max and Lila, so your mum and dad can have some time together. And your grandpa wants to get on with those new plants he's bought. Shall we take this clever little dog with us, hmmm?" She patted Rascal on the head, and Ellie made a thumbs up sign at Rascal. He was finally winning Gran over!

The cove was about a mile along the beach, but with the picnic and the rugs and all the swimming things to carry, it felt much further. Everyone was hot by the time they got there, and Gran pointed out that it would be best to swim while the tide was coming in, so they all ran into the sea, even Gran, leaving Rascal standing worriedly by the edge of the water.

"Come on, come with us," Ellie called, but he just ran up and down the shoreline, looking worried.

"Some dogs just don't like water, Ellie," Gran told her.

"He tried to drink it," Ellie told Gran, as

they swam a little further out. "And he got splashed by a wave the other day. I think he's a bit scared of the sea now."

"Just don't let him bury the towels again!" Lila called.

"He won't," Ellie told her, looking back at Rascal. "He's gone to sit on the rug. He's fine. Just sitting next to the picnic bag."

Gran looked round sharply. "Is he?"

Ellie peered over at Rascal. "Yes. Um... I'd better go back and check on him..."

There was something shiny hanging out of Rascal's mouth. Something that looked awfully like the foil Gran had wrapped the sandwiches in.

"Rascal! No!" Ellie half swam, half splashed her way out of the water, to find

My Naughty Little Puppy

Rascal happily demolishing a whole packet of sandwiches. Ham ... his favourite!

And Gran was right behind her, looking furious.

Chapter Eight

Cave Adventure

"Take him for a walk up the beach and get him out of Gran's way," Lila muttered. "You too, Max, go on."

Ellie slipped on her flip-flops and hustled Rascal away. Gran was checking the picnic bag to see if Rascal had eaten anything else.

"Let's go and look at those rocks over by the cliff." Max pointed along the beach. "That's far enough away to get Rascal out of Gran's sight."

My Naughty Little Puppy

Ellie nodded. She clipped on Rascal's
lead and they hurried down the beach. The
rocks were piled up against the cliff just at
the edge of the bay.

Even though they were only exploring
to keep Rascal and Gran apart, Ellie soon
found herself amazed at the little damp

crevices between the rocks – full of shells, and different seaweeds, and tiny crabs that disappeared as soon as Rascal stuck his nose into their holes.

"This is really cool," Max said, clambering to the top of another big rock. "Oh, wow, look! There's a cave!"

They had been working their way towards the cliff face itself, and now Ellie saw that Max was right. It was a narrow little crevice, damp and dark, and she watched as Max climbed speedily over the rocks towards the entrance. "I'm not sure we should go in there," she called nervously, but Max was already standing in the opening, not listening to her.

"It goes back really far! And I reckon it must go through to a hole or something up above, because there's some light coming in further down."

Ellie and Rascal followed him, slipping and scrambling over the rocks. Somehow when Max said there was light, it made Ellie feel better – she'd been scared of going into somewhere dark and eerie. Feeling a little bit silly, she stood hesitating at the entrance, but Rascal was keen to follow Max, and pulled on his lead. He obviously didn't think the cave was scary.

"There might be treasure!" Max called back, and Ellie grinned. Max had been obsessed with pirates until a couple of years ago, and it looked like he hadn't really grown out of it after all.

"Is it safe?" she shouted back, and Max snorted. "Of course it is! It would be fenced off if it wasn't."

Ellie nodded. That was probably true. She stepped into the dim, salty air of the cave, and followed Max, who was quite far ahead now. It wasn't at all like she'd

My Naughty Little Puppy

imagined – no slime dripping down the walls and definitely no skeletons. Just walls of crumbling greyish-brown rock. The sandy floor was covered in shells, swept in by the sea, and Ellie peered at them in the greyish light. She was sure that there were some kinds she'd never seen before, and she hunted through them eagerly. She'd found lots for Christy's present, but she was sure that these were some of the nicest.

Ellie let Rascal off the lead. He sniffed around the cave, his paws scratching and scrabbling on the rocks, then returned to the entrance. He stood there for a few minutes, and then Ellie heard him whine. She looked up. "What's the matter, Rascal?"

He whined again, staring out at the rocks. Ellie went to see what Rascal was looking at, and gasped. "Max! Max, quick! The tide's coming in!"

Max dashed back down the cave, stumbling in the darkness, and looked out at the water lapping up around the rocks.

"What are we going to do?" Ellie cried.

"It's OK, Ellie," Max said calmly. "We can go back to the other end, and climb out through the hole. Hey, don't be scared."

Ellie nodded, and they hurried to the other end of the cave where a pile of rocks had fallen, leaving a big hole in the ceiling.

"I'm not sure I can get up there with Rascal," Ellie said nervously, staring up at the tricky-looking climb.

Max frowned. "Maybe you're right. Oh, well. We'll just have to go for a paddle!"

It was all very well for Max to say that, Ellie realized as she watched him step out of the hole in the cliff and balance carefully on the nearest rock, but persuading Rascal was another matter entirely. He'd had quite enough of the sea this week. When Ellie clipped his lead back on, and prepared to make the wobbly scramble on to the rock, Rascal started to howl and wriggled

My Naughty Little Puppy

backwards, trying to pull himself out of
his collar.

"Rascal, come on!" Ellie coaxed.

"What's the problem?" Max clambered
back to them. "We need to hurry, or we're
going to get soaked."

My Naughty Little Puppy

"I can't make Rascal move!" Ellie told him. "He won't budge."

Max grabbed the puppy round the middle, and carried him, howling and wriggling, across the rocks. The water had risen up around them, so it was like hopping from one tiny island to another. They were

My Naughty Little Puppy

just reaching the last of the rocks, when Ellie
saw Gran and Lila hurrying down the
beach towards them, waving.

"Are you all right?" Gran called. "We've
been looking everywhere for you; we
thought you must have gone along the cliff
path at the top."

"We found a cave," Max yelled back. "We were inside, we didn't see the tide coming in. Sorry, Gran!"

"You'll have to wade across this last bit," Lila called.

She and Gran were standing on the beach, between the cliff edge and the creeping tide. Lila pulled off her jewelled sandals, and started to walk through the water towards the rocks. It seemed to get deep awfully quickly – she was up to her knees, and she wasn't even halfway to Max and Ellie.

Max looked round at Ellie, shouting over Rascal's panicky howls. "Ellie, you have to just slip down the side of the rock. Feel for the sea bed with your feet, OK?"

My Naughty Little Puppy

Ellie nodded, and watched as Max wriggled down into the water - it was up to his waist! Rascal struggled in Max's arms, howling, and then clawed his way up on to Max's shoulder, where he sat draped round Max's neck like a little furry scarf. She giggled. Poor Rascal. He really didn't like the sea!

Ellie slid down the rock, and gasped as she landed in the cold water. "Shh, shh, Rascal!" she murmured - or she tried to, but her teeth were chattering. She reached out for Max's hand, and they waded through the water to Lila.

"We were starting to get worried," Gran told them, giving Ellie a hug as Lila helped her out of the water.

My Naughty Little Puppy

Ellie lifted Rascal off Max's shoulders.
He was whimpering miserably. "Not as
worried as Rascal!"

Gran tickled Rascal's ears. "Come on,
poor little pup. This time I'll actually *give* you
a ham sandwich."

Chapter Nine

The Terrible Tea Party

Gran didn't make a big fuss about Ellie and Max's adventure to Mum and Dad, when they got back from their outing, although she did make the two of them promise to take more care with the tides. But at least Rascal seemed to be back in Gran's good books again. She even let Ellie show off Rascal's tricks to her while she was baking another of her lovely cakes – sitting, and staying, and not eating his dog treat until he was told.

My Naughty Little Puppy

"What a good dog! You can show him
off to my friends from jigsaw club this
afternoon, Ellie. They're coming round for
tea and cake. We're working on a huge
puzzle at the moment, two thousand
pieces. But we've nearly finished it."

Gran looked at Ellie thoughtfully. "You'd
better go and change, dear. Those are the
shorts you had on earlier, aren't they?
They're looking a bit sandy."

Ellie took the hint, and went upstairs to
change into a skirt. She persuaded Max
to change too, and Lila didn't need any
persuading. All three of them looked
immaculate by the time the jigsaw ladies
arrived – and Ellie had even brushed
Rascal.

My Naughty Little Puppy

"Oh, isn't he lovely?" all the ladies
cooed, and Rascal sat under the dining
table as they did their jigsaw, looking
angelic and nibbling the pieces of cake that
kept being handed down to him.

My Naughty Little Puppy

Ellie was curled up on the sofa, enjoying reading after their adventurous morning, when she noticed that the happy buzz of chatter round the jigsaw had stopped.

"I don't understand it..." Gran murmured. "I rolled this jigsaw up in its special mat, and it's been safe in the cupboard since last week. We simply can't have lost a piece."

Ellie put down her book, feeling worried. Things did tend to disappear when Rascal was around. She leaned over the arm of the sofa, and peered under the table.

Rascal came out to meet her, wagging his tail – and spat out something small and greyish. Something that might once have been the missing last piece of the two-thousand piece jigsaw...

My Naughty Little Puppy

"I've put him out in the garden, Gran," Ellie said, in a small voice. "I'm very sorry..."

The jigsaw ladies had all gone home, leaving Gran crossly doing the washing up.

"We'll go and buy a replacement jigsaw tomorrow." Mum sounded really embarrassed. "Er, shall I make some tea?"

"I'd love some," said Grandad, stepping through the kitchen door and wiping his muddy shoes on the mat.

Ellie went into the living room, to keep out of Gran's way. Grandad put on a film for her, but Ellie couldn't stop thinking about Rascal. Finally, she sneaked into the kitchen to go and play in the garden with him.

She closed the door carefully behind her and looked around the garden, expecting Rascal to come running over. But there was no joyful bark to greet her.

"Rascal!" Ellie called, and then a little louder. She searched the garden, starting to feel the tiniest bit worried. Still no puppy. She checked down the side path, to see if he'd gone round into the front. He couldn't have jumped over the wall, could he? Gran had been very cross and told him off. Could that have made him run away?

Ellie hurried down the path, then gasped in horror. The front gate was wide open, and the garden was empty!

Chapter Ten

The Great Rascal Hunt

Ellie dashed out on to the pavement, hoping to find Rascal doing something awful like digging up next door's garden. She didn't care what he was doing, as long as he was safe.

"Rascal! Rascal!" She looked down the street in both directions, but couldn't see him at all. Trying not to cry, she raced back into the house, yelling for Mum and Dad, Lila and Max. "Rascal's gone! The gate was open, and he's disappeared! I can't see him anywhere!"

Mum was sitting at the dining table, looking guiltily at the jigsaw, with its telltale missing piece. She jumped up, nearly upsetting her tea over the rest of the puzzle. "Oh no, Ellie, are you sure? He isn't anywhere in the garden?"

"I've checked!" Ellie wailed. "Someone must have left the gate open. We have to go and find him!"

Dad was already at the front door, pulling on his shoes. "And his collar's got our home number on, not the mobile. Come on, Ellie. Where would he have headed?"

Ellie followed him down the path, with Mum, Max, Lila and Gran and Grandpa hurrying after them.

"He likes the beach, doesn't he, Ellie?" Grandpa suggested.

Ellie nodded. "But he loved it when we went shopping too – people kept stroking him. And that little girl gave him the end of her ice cream cone on the pier. He might have gone anywhere!"

"We'd better split up," Dad said. "Ellie, you come with me, we'll go to the beach. Max and Grandpa go and check the pier. Lila, you and Mum and Gran go along the high street."

Ellie and Dad hurried down the street to the cliff steps. They could see a long way down the beach, but there was no Rascal rooting about in his favourite

seaweed piles. It was hard to tell, though.
There were so many people on the beach,
with windbreaks, and even little tents. Rascal
could be anywhere.

They hurried down the steps, and ran
into the red-haired boys with the Westie at
the bottom. "You haven't seen my puppy,
have you?" Ellie gasped out. "Rascal?
My Jack Russell?"

The red-haired boys frowned. "No...
Has he run off? We'll keep an eye out
for him."

"Thanks!" Ellie called, hurrying away
down the sand.

Dad and Ellie stopped lots of other
people, but no one had seen a white dog
with brown patches. It was odd how many
people said things like, "Oh, the little Jack
Russell puppy?" when they asked – Rascal
seemed to have charmed everyone they'd
met on their walks.

They ran along the beach, asking
everyone they met. Ellie was running so fast
she started to feel sick. And the smell of fish
and chips wafting down from the top of the
cliff only made her feel worse.

My Naughty Little Puppy

She stopped suddenly, grabbing Dad's hand. "Fish and chips! I bet he's gone to the fish and chip shop! I can smell it, and I bet he could too."

She dashed over to the nearest steps, racing up them two at a time.

"Ellie!" It was Max and Grandpa, hurrying along the cliff path.

"He wasn't at the pier then?" Ellie asked.

"No, but then we thought of the fish and chip shop. When I took him out yesterday before bed, he headed straight for it," Max explained.

Ellie nodded. "We thought so too. Let's go and see."

"Oh, isn't he cute? Look at him begging!"

"I wonder who he belongs to?"

Ellie could hear the cooing voices even before she saw Rascal, sitting next to a family at one of the tables, doing his best starving puppy face. "Rascal!" she cried.

He trotted towards her, and Ellie swept him up in her arms, laughing and crying all at once. "I thought we'd lost you!"

Rascal licked her enthusiastically, and he smelled of chips. Then he looked hopefully back at the table, obviously wondering if he could have more.

Ellie laughed into his fur as she saw Mum and Lila and Gran hurrying towards them. It looked like everyone had thought of Rascal and chips! "We'll ask Mum, OK? Maybe a few. Just please don't ever run off like that again, Rascal!"

Rascal wagged his tail, and Ellie was sure it was his way of saying sorry.

Pooch Parley!

 Your pet pooch can't talk to you (though you swear he understands you sometimes!) but he does have special ways to communicate with you and other dogs.

Dogs sniff each others' bottoms as a greeting and to find out more about each other. It's like shaking hands to us!

Woof! Woof! Woof!

Dogs use their tails to show how happy they are. A dog behaviour expert invented "the wagometer" to judge whether it's a fast, excited wag meaning "I'm happy", or a wag that means "Don't come close"!

Hounds sniff everything, everywhere – they're making a mental map of who has been there before them.

Beagles and collies are the noisiest dogs! They were bred to chase and scare other animals, and let their owners know where the animals were.

Your toothy smile means you're happy, but to a dog it can look like you're baring your teeth and ready to attack!

🐾 Dogs can be as clever as a toddler – they understand up to 200 words, and can even count to five!

🐾 Border collies are the smartest – a dog called Chaser in the USA knows over a thousand words!

🐾 Think your dog is howling at the moon to wake you up? Dogs are like wolves, they howl to communicate to others far away. If your pooch howls when you've left the house, he's calling for you to come back!

🐾 Dogs have facial expressions, just like us! They prick up their ears when alert, raise their eyebrows when interested or confused, and even yawn when they're bored!

🐾 In English, dogs go "woof woof!", in Mandarin Chinese the noise is "wang wang!", in Italian, it's "bau bau!" and the Indonesians use "guk guk!".

🐾 The Basenji, an African breed of dog, yodels instead of barking!

Coming soon

The Christmas holidays are here and better still, it's snowing! Ellie plans to take Rascal carol singing – in his cute Santa hat they're bound to raise loads of money for charity! But wherever Rascal goes, trouble is never far behind...

Out now:

Holly Webb

My
Naughty
Little
Puppy

A Home
for Rascal

The Thomas family are
finally getting a puppy –
and no one is more excited
than dog-mad Ellie!
She dreams of a cuddly
little pup who will sleep
on her bed. But her bossy
older brother and sister
have other ideas. Will Ellie
get her perfect puppy?

Rascal's naughtiness
is annoying the whole family,
and Ellie isn't sure what to do.
So when Grandad suggests
puppy-training classes, she
can't wait to get started.
It's time for Ellie to teach
Rascal some new tricks!
But things don't go quite
as planned...

Out now:

School Sports Day is coming up, and Ellie is worried she'll be last at everything. But then she comes up with an excellent idea – she can practise for the events with Rascal! After all, the playful puppy is far better at running and catching things than she is. Can Rascal save the day?

Out now:

Holly Webb

My Naughty Little Puppy

Rascal's Sleepover Fun

It's Ellie's birthday soon,
and she'd love to have a
sleepover party. She knows
that Rascal would love one
too! But Mum isn't so keen,
and Ellie and Rascal will need
to be on their best behaviour
to get her to say yes.
Will Rascal stay out of trouble
long enough for Ellie to
have her perfect party?